Bridges

Ken Robbins
Bridges

DIAL BOOKS  NEW YORK

For Sam Taylor

Thanks to John Okrent for his help.

Published by Dial Books, A Division of Penguin Books USA Inc.
375 Hudson Street, New York, New York 10014

Copyright © 1991 by Ken Robbins · All rights reserved
Design by Amelia Lau Carling
Printed in the U.S.A.
First Edition
1 3 5 7 9 10 8 6 4 2

Library of Congress Cataloging in Publication Data
Robbins, Ken. Bridges / by Ken Robbins.
p. cm.
Summary: Hand-colored photographs illustrate bridges of many
different types, with descriptions of their design and use.
ISBN 0-8037-0929-3.—ISBN 0-8037-0930-7 (lib. bdg.)
1. Bridges—Juvenile literature. [1. Bridges.] I. Title.
TG148.R63 1991 624'.2—dc20 90-35776 CIP AC

The art reproduced in this book was created from original black-and-white
photographs that were hand colored by the author.

Author's Note

I have always been impressed by the beauty and ingenuity
of bridges. To my mind they reflect everything
bold, ambitious, and strong about human nature.

Bridges shorten our journey and ease our way.
Many kinds have been built over the centuries,
each suited to a special purpose and place—from a simple
wooden footbridge across a quiet creek to an immense
steel suspension bridge soaring high above a mile-wide river.

The photographs in this book show a number of different
bridges. They may vary in the ways they are built,
but great or small; wooden, steel, or stone; bridges enhance
and expand our world by joining one place with another.

Ken Robbins
East Hampton, New York
February 1991

A log across a small creek is the simplest kind of bridge. It must be long enough to reach from one bank to the other, as well as strong enough to carry the weight of a person. This simple span has just one part, the tree, though most bridges have many. Engineers call the parts members, because like the members of a team they work together to make the bridge strong.

A larger stream calls for a bigger bridge;
a heavier load needs a stronger one. Travelers would have
to go many miles out of their way if it weren't for this bridge.
The diagonal members in criss-cross patterns
are called trusses. They make the bridge strong enough
to carry automobiles and trucks.

A railroad bridge across a large waterway must bear
enormous weight. The steel members of this bridge are
formed into a semicircular shape called an arch.
Graceful, beautiful, and especially strong, the arch
is used in many bridges and in buildings too.

Although many bridges cross over water,
some cross over roads instead. This is another type of
arch bridge; but this one crosses a parkway and is made of stone.
Bridges over highways are sometimes called overpasses
because they allow one road to pass over another.

Sometimes bridges are built where they are not really needed. You could easily jump or even step over the tiny little stream this footbridge crosses. Built more for convenience and pleasure than necessity, its beautiful handcrafted features reflect the serenity of its surroundings.

Covered bridges were once common in places where
snowfalls were heavy. In the days when these bridges were built
there was no steel for construction. But the weight of
piled up snow was often too much for a wooden bridge to bear.
So the bridges were built with peaked roofs, not to protect the
traveler, but to protect the bridges by letting the snow slide off.
This bridge is almost 150 years old and still used today.

There are other kinds of covered bridges,
built for different reasons. Made of metal and glass,
this bridge crosses not a river but a busy street. It lets people
walk from one office building to another,
saving time and effort while protecting them
from weather and the dangers of city traffic.

Drawbridges are designed to move—usually to allow
tall boats to pass underneath them. Some drawbridges contain
one or more hinged sections that can be raised.
Medieval castles often had moats around them
with drawbridges that could be raised to keep enemies out.

Another kind of drawbridge, the vertical lift,
has two towers with a section of bridge between them
that can be raised straight up. This vertical lift is a train bridge
over a canal. Because trains don't come by very frequently
and many boats use the canal, the bridge usually rests in the raised
position. When a train must cross, boat traffic is stopped
and the bridge is lowered just long enough for the train to pass.

Elevated highways often go on for miles and miles.
They may not seem to be crossing anything in particular,
but there is always a reason why they have been built.
Sometimes it's to avoid destroying homes in an area where
a road is needed. In this case it's because the land below
is marshy and wet. The ground is too soft to support
a regular highway, and the elevated road is less damaging
to the delicate environment of the marshlands.

Suspension bridges are roadways in the sky.
They hang in the air, held up by cables attached to very high towers
or anchored to the ground on either side of the bridge.
This long, elegant suspension bridge is more than a mile
from end to end and contains thousands of miles of wires—
some of which are woven into cables almost three feet thick.

Very often a bridge will be built with a number of materials in a combination of styles. This bridge is made of steel and stone. Like a truss bridge, it has criss-crossed members to make it stronger, and like a suspension bridge it hangs from tall towers.

Bridges play a useful part in everyone's life.
In major cities and small towns and even in the wilderness,
they carry people, vehicles, and goods over
gorges and streams, rivers and roads. But bridges are more
than just practical structures. They are monuments to craft and
imagination, to technology and beauty, and to our need
to reach beyond the boundaries of nature.

The photograph appearing on the front cover is the Manhattan Bridge,
connecting Brooklyn and Manhattan in New York.
The back cover photograph shows the Newburgh-Beacon Bridge,
which connects Newburgh and Beacon in New York.